# Horror Stories

# DR JEKYLL AND MR HYDE

## Robert Louis Stevenson

abridged edition

# The Story of the Door

Mr Utterson the lawyer was a man of rugged countenance that was never lighted by a smile, and yet he was somehow lovable. It was frequently his fortune to be the last reputable acquaintance and the last good influence in the lives of down-going men. And to such as these, so long as they came about in his chambers, he never marked a shade of change in his demeanour. No doubt this was easy to Mr Utterson, for he was undemonstrative at best. His friends were those whom he had known the longest; his affections were a growth of time, they implied no aptness in the subject. Hence the bond that united him to Mr Richard Enfield, his distant kinsman and a well-known man about town, whom he accompanied on Sunday walks.

On one such walk, they happened to wander down a by-street in a busy quarter of London, a street which showed that all its inhabitants seemed to be doing well, for it exhibited well-painted shutters, well-polished brasses and a general cleanliness and gaiety of tone. Two doors from the corner, the line was broken by the entry of a court, and just at that point a certain sinister building thrust its gable into the street. There was a door in the wall, equipped with neither bell nor knocker, whose paint was blistered and stained. Tramps slouched in the recess and struck matches on the wood, a schoolboy had tried his knife on it, and no one appeared to have these people driven away to repair the damage.

Mr Enfield pointed at the door, and announced that it was connected with a very odd story he had to tell.

"I was coming home at about three o'clock on a black winter morning, when there seemed to be nothing to be seen but street lamps. All at once I saw two figures, one a little man who was stumping along eastward at a good walk, and the other a little girl who was running as hard as she could down a cross street. The two ran into one another naturally enough at the corner, and then came the horrible part of it, for the man trampled calmly over the child's body and left her screaming and writhing on the ground. It was hellish to see, not like a man but like some Juggernaut. I gave a shout, ran after him and dragged him back to where there was already quite a group around her. He was perfectly cool and gave no resistance, but gave me one look, so ugly that it brought out the sweat on me. The crowd consisted of the girl's family, and pretty soon the doctor for whom she had been sent arrived. There was little wrong with her except shock, but there was one curious circumstance. I had loathed the man on sight, and so had the child's family, which was only natural. But the doctor's case struck me – he was the normal cut and dry apothecary, with a strong Edinburgh accent, and about as emotional as a bagpipe. But every time he looked at my prisoner, I saw that he turned sick and white with the desire to kill him. We told the man we could and would make such a scandal out of this, as should make his name stink from one end of London to the other. If he had any friends or any credit, we undertook that he should lose them. And all the time, as we were pitching it in red hot, we were keeping the women off him as best we could, for they were as wild as harpies. I never saw such a circle of hateful faces: and there was the man in the middle, with a kind of black, sneering coolness – frightened too, I could see that – but carrying it off, sir, really like Satan. 'If you choose to make capital out of this incident,' said he, 'I am naturally helpless. No gentleman but wishes to avoid a scene,' says he. 'Name your figure.' We insisted that the family should be compensated for the hurt to the child, and fixed on a sum of one hundred pounds. The man agreed, and where do you think he led us but to that door? He whipped out a key, went in and returned with a cheque for the amount, made payable to bearer, and signed with a name I can't mention, though it's one of the points of my story, but it was a name very well known and often printed. The signature was good for more than the sum asked, if it was genuine, but as I pointed out to him, it seemed foolish for us to accept a cheque from one man signed with the name of another. He stayed with us, the doctor and myself, until the banks opened, and although I said at the bank that I thought it might be forged, it was not."

He added that since then he had privately called the place with the door Black Mail House, for it seemed that the well-known person who drew the cheque must have been blackmailed by this sinister fellow for some youthful indiscretion. Mr Utterson asked rather suddenly, "And you don't know if the drawer of the cheque lives there?"

"A likely place, isn't it?" returned Mr Enfield. "But I happen to have noticed his address; he lives in some square or other."

"And you never asked about – the place with the door?" said Mr Utterson.

"No, sir, I had a delicacy," was the reply. "I feel very strongly about putting questions; it partakes too much of the style of the day of judgment. You start a question, and it's like starting a stone. You sit quietly on the top of a hill, and away the stone goes, starting others; and presently some bland old bird (the last you would have thought of) is knocked on the head in his own back garden, and the family have to change their name. No, sir, I make it a golden rule of mine: the more it looks like Queer Street, the less I ask."

"A very good rule too," said the lawyer.

Mr Enfield said that he had studied the place for himself, and had drawn the conclusion that someone must live there, for there was a chimney that was generally smoking, and the few windows that were there were clean, but he could not be too sure because the buildings were so tightly packed together that it was hard to say where one ended and the next began.

"There's one point I wish to ask," said Mr Utterson, as the pair walked on. "What was the name of the man who walked over the child?"

"Hyde," responded Mr Enfield. "He is not easy to describe. There is something wrong with his appearance, something displeasing, something downright detestable. I never saw a man I so disliked, and yet I scarce know why. He must be deformed somewhere, he gives the strong impression of deformity, although I couldn't specify the point. An extraordinary-looking man, and yet I can really name nothing out of the way. I can't describe him, but it's not for want of memory, for I can see him this moment."

"You are sure he used a key?" asked Mr Utterson again. "I know it must seem strange to ask again, but you see, Richard, if I do not ask you the name of the other person, it is because I know it already. Your tale has gone home."

"I have been pedantically exact," replied his companion. "The fellow had a key and has it still — I saw him use it not a week ago."

Mr Utterson sighed deeply.

"Let us make a bargain," said the younger man, seeing this, "never to speak more about this matter."

"With all my heart," said the lawyer.

# The Search for Mr Hyde

That evening, Mr Utterson went home in sombre spirits. As soon as he had dined, without relish, he took up a candle and went to his business room. There he opened his safe, took out a document endorsed on the envelope as the will of Dr Jekyll, and sat down to study its contents. This will provided not only that in case of the decease of Henry Jekyll, all his possessions were to pass into the hands of his "friend and benefactor Edward Hyde", but that in the case of Dr Jekyll's "disappearance or unexplained absence for any period exceeding three calendar months", the said Edward Hyde should step into Henry Jekyll's shoes straight away. This document had long been an eyesore to the lawyer. Hitherto, it had been ignorance of Mr Hyde that had swelled his indignation – now it was his knowledge.

Soon, he blew out his candle and went to visit his friend the great Dr Lanyon who would know anything there was to know about the mysterious Mr Hyde. The solemn butler knew him and welcomed him: he was subjected to no stage of delay, but ushered direct from the door to the dining room, where Dr Lanyon sat alone over his wine. This was a hearty, healthy, dapper. red-faced gentleman, with a shock of hair prematurely white, and with a boisterous and decided manner. At sight of Mr Utterson, he sprang up from his chair and welcomed him with

both hands. The geniality, as was the way of the man, was somewhat theatrical to the eye; but it reposed on genuine feeling. For these two were old friends, old mates both at school and college, both thorough respecters of themselves and of each other, and what does not always follow, men who thoroughly enjoyed each other's company. After a little rambling talk, the lawyer led up to the subject.

"I suppose," he said, "that you and I, Lanyon, must be Henry Jekyll's two oldest friends."

"Yes, I suppose we are," agreed Dr Lanyon. "And what of that? I see little of him now."

"Indeed!" rejoined Utterson. "I thought you had a bond of common interest."

"We did," was the reply. "But it is more than ten years since Henry Jekyll became too fanciful for me. He began to go wrong – wrong in mind, and although I have continued to take an interest in him, I have seen devilish little of the man. Such unscientific balderdash," added the doctor, flushing suddenly purple, "would have estranged Damon and Pythias."

"Did you ever meet his protege, Edward Hyde?" asked Utterson.

"Hyde? No, never heard of him," replied Lanyon shortly.

Utterson spent a restless night thinking of the mysterious Hyde. As he lay and tossed in the darkness of the night and the curtained room, Mr Enfield's tale went by before his mind in a scroll of lighted pictures. He would be aware of the great

14

field of lamps of a nocturnal city; then of the figure of a man walking swiftly; then of a child running; and then these met, and that human Juggernaut trod the child down and passed on regardless of her screams. Or else he would see a room in a rich house, where his friend lay asleep, dreaming and smiling in his dreams and then the door of that room would be opened, the curtains of the bed plucked apart, the sleeper recalled, and lo! there would stand by his side a figure to whom power was given, and even at that dead hour, he must rise and do its bidding. The figure in these two phases haunted the lawyer all night, and if at any time he dozed over, it was but to see it glide more swiftly and still the more swiftly, even to dizziness, through wilder labyrinths of lamp-lighted city, and at every street corner crush a child and leave her screaming. And still the figure had no face by which he might know it; even in his dreams it had no face, or one that baffled him and melted before his eyes; and thus it was that there sprang up and grew apace in the lawyer's mind a singularly strong, almost inordinate, curiosity to behold the features of the real Mr Hyde. If he could but once set eyes on him, he thought the mystery would lighten and perhaps roll altogether away, as was the habit of mysterious things when well examined. He might see a reason for his friend's strange preference or bondage (call it which you please), and even for the startling clauses of the will. And at least it would be a face worth seeing: the face of a man who was without bowels of pity: a face which had but to show itself to raise in the unimpressionable Enfield a spirit of enduring hatred.

From that time on he began to haunt the street where the building with the door was, and at last his patience was rewarded. Late one night, he caught sight of a small figure making its way towards the door, and as he approached it Mr Utterson stepped out and touched him on the shoulder.

"Mr Hyde, I think?"

Hyde shrank back with a hissing breath, but although he did not look the lawyer in the face, he answered coolly enough, "That is my name. What do you want?"

"I see you are going in," said the lawyer. "I am an old friend of Dr Jekyll's – Mr Utterson of Gaunt Street – you must have heard my name. Meeting you so conveniently, I thought you might admit me."

"Dr Jekyll is not at home," replied the other.

"Will you do me the favour of allowing me to see your face?" asked Mr Utterson. The pair stared at one another rather fixedly for a few seconds.

"Now I will know you again," said the lawyer.

Mr Hyde agreed, saying it was as well that they had met, and gave him his address. "And now," he said, "how did you know me?"

"We have common friends," said Mr Utterson.

The other snarled aloud into a savage laugh,

and the next moment had unlocked the door and vanished into the house.

Left alone, Mr Utterson thought about the man. Mr Hyde was pale and dwarfish. He gave an impression of deformity without any nameable malformation, he had a displeasing smile, a manner of a sort of murderous mixture of timidity and boldness, and he spoke with a husky, whispering and somewhat broken voice. But not all of these together could explain the disgust, loathing and fear which Mr Utterson had felt on regarding him.

"There is something else," said the perplexed gentleman. "There must be something else, if I could find a name for it. God bless me, the man seemed hardly human. Something troglodytic, shall we say? or can it be the old story of Doctor Fell? or is it the mere radiance of a foul soul that transpires through thus, and transfigures, its clay continent? The last, I think, for, O my poor old Harry Jekyll, if ever I read Satan's signature upon a face, it is on that of your new friend."

Round the corner was a square of ancient, handsome houses, now somewhat decayed. One house, however, was still occupied entirely, and gave forth a great air of wealth and comfort. Mr Utterson stopped here and knocked.

A well-dressed elderly servant opened the door.

"Is Dr Jekyll at home, Poole?" asked the lawyer.

"I will see, Mr Utterson," responded the butler,

and admitted the visitor to the hall. Presently Poole returned to inform him that Dr Jekyll was out.

"I saw Mr Hyde go in by the old dissecting-room door," said Utterson. "Is that right, when Dr Jekyll is out?"

"Quite right, Mr Utterson, sir," responded the servant. "Mr Hyde has a key, and we all have orders to obey him."

"I do not think I ever met Mr Hyde?"

"Oh no, sir, he never dines here. Indeed we rarely see him on this side of the house – he comes and goes by the laboratory."

"Well, good night, Poole," said the lawyer, and took his leave with a heavy heart. Surely the presence of Hyde in Harry Jekyll's house was the result of some old sin committed by a younger Jekyll – maybe he was being blackmailed by him for some ancient iniquity. Hyde must have black secrets of his own, compared to which Jekyll's must be like sunshine. Things could not continue as they were. It turned Utterson cold to think of Hyde existing in the same house as Jekyll – for if he once came to discover the strange clauses of Harry Jekyll's will, he might well decide to speed along his inheritance.

"Ah," he thought, "I must put my shoulder to the wheel – if Jekyll will let me."

And once more before his mind's eye he saw the strange clauses of the will.

# Dr Jekyll was Quite at Ease

A fortnight later, by some excellent chance, the doctor gave one of his pleasant dinners to some five or six old cronies, and Mr Utterson so contrived that he remained behind after the others had all departed. This was no new arrangement, but a thing that had befallen many scores of time. Where Mr Utterson was liked he was liked well, and Dr Jekyll was no exception to this, as he now sat on the other side of the fireplace, a large, well-made, smooth-faced man of fifty, with a slyish cast perhaps, but every mark of friendship and kindness on his face – you could see by his looks that he cherished for Mr Utterson a sincere and warm affection.

"I have been wanting to speak to you," began the lawyer. "You know that will of yours?"

A close observer might have gathered that the subject was distasteful, but the doctor carried it off gaily. "My poor Utterson," he said. "You are unfortunate in such a client. I never saw a man so distressed by my will as you are – unless it was Lanyon at what he called my scientific heresies."

"You know I never approved of your will," pursued Mr Utterson, refusing to be led away from the subject.

"Yes, certainly I know that," said the doctor, a trifle sharply.

"Well, I tell you so again. I have been learning

19

something of Mr Hyde."

The large handsome face of Dr Jekyll grew pale to the very lips, and there came a blackness about his eyes. "I do not care to hear more," he said.

"What I heard was abominable," said Utterson.

"It can make no change," said the doctor. "You do not understand my position. I am painfully situated, Utterson, my position is a very strange one indeed. It is one of those affairs that cannot be mended by talking."

"Jekyll," said Utterson. "You know me. I am a man to be trusted. Make a clean breast of this in confidence, and I make no doubt I can get you out of it."

"My good Utterson," said the doctor, "this is very good of you, and I cannot find words enough to thank you. I believe you fully, I would trust you before any other man alive – but indeed it isn't what you fancy. It is not so bad as that. And just to put your good heart at rest, I will tell you one thing – the moment I choose I can get rid of Mr Hyde. I give you my hand upon that. I will just add one little word, Utterson. This is a private matter, and I beg of you to let it sleep."

"I have no doubt you are perfectly right," said Utterson, looking into the fire.

"I have really a great interest in Hyde," continued the doctor. "I know you have seen him – he told me so, and I fear he was rude. But I do sincerely take a great interest in that young man, and if I am taken away, Utterson, I wish you to promise me that you will bear with him and get his rights for him. It would be a weight off my mind if you would promise."

"I can't pretend that I shall ever like him," said the lawyer.

"I don't ask that," pleaded Jekyll, laying his hand on the other's arm. "I only ask you to help him for my sake when I am no longer here."

Utterson heaved a sigh. "Well," he said, "I promise."

## The Carew Murder Case

Nearly a year later, London was startled by a crime of singular ferocity, and rendered all the more notable by the high position of the victim.

A maidservant living alone in a house not far from the river had gone to bed at about eleven. It seems she was romantically inclined, for she was sitting by the window and had fallen into a dream of musing. As she sat there she became aware of an aged and beautiful gentleman with white hair drawing near along the lane, and advancing to meet him another and a very small gentleman, to whom she at first paid less attention. When they had come within speech, which was just under her window, the older man bowed and addressed the other with a pretty manner of politeness, merely asking him directions. The maidservant watched him for a moment, as his face seemed to breathe such an innocent and old-world kindliness of disposition. Presently her eye wandered to the other, and she was surprised to recognise him as Mr Hyde, who had once visited her master and for whom she had conceived a dislike. He had in his hand a heavy cane, and he answered never a word and seemed to listen with an ill-contained impatience. And then of a sudden he broke out in a great flame of temper, brandishing the cane as though he were a madman. The old gentleman took a step backwards, very surprised and a trifle hurt, and at that Mr Hyde clubbed him to the earth with his cane. Next moment, with ape-like fury, he was trampling his victim under foot and hailing down a storm of blows, under which the bones were audibly shattered and the body bounced on the roadway. At the horror of this, the maid fainted.

It was two o'clock when she recovered and called for the police. The murderer had long since vanished, but the victim was there, and half of the cane with which the foul deed had been done, and although it was of very tough and heavy wood, the stick had broken in the middle. A purse and gold watch were found upon the victim, and a sealed and stamped envelope, addressed to Mr Utterson.

This was brought to the lawyer the next morning, and he was asked to come at once and identify the body.

"Yes," he said. "I recognise him. It is the body of Sir Danvers Carew."

The officer with him quickly told him what had

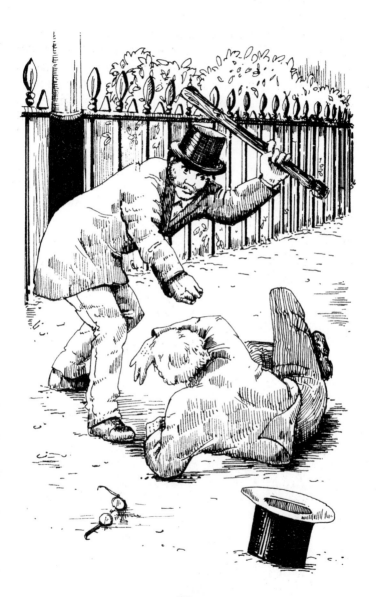

happened, and showed him the broken stick. Utterson, who had already quailed at the name of Hyde, could doubt no longer when the stick was shown him. Battered and broken as it was, he recognised it at once as one he had himself given to Harry Jekyll many years before.

"Is Mr Hyde a person of low stature?" he asked.

"Particularly small and evil-looking, is what the maid calls him," rejoined the officer.

Mr Utterson reflected for a moment. "I think I can take you to his house," he said. It was by this time about nine in the morning, and the first fog of the season. A great chocolate-coloured pall lowered over heaven, but the wind was continually charging and routing these embattled vapours; so that as the cab crawled from street to street, Mr Utterson beheld a marvellous number of degrees and hues of twilight; for here it would be dark like the back-end of evening; and there would be a glow of a rich, lurid brown, like the light of some strange conflagration: and here, for a moment, the fog would be quite broken up, and a haggard shaft of daylight would glance in between these swirling wreaths. The dismal quarter of Soho seen under these changing glimpses, with its muddy ways and slatternly passengers, and its lamps, which had never been extinguished or had been kindled afresh to combat this mournful reinvasion of darkness, seemed in the lawyer's eyes like a district of some city in a nightmare. The thoughts of his mind, besides, were of the gloomiest dye;

and when he glanced at the companion of his drive, he was conscious of some touch of the terror which may at times assail the most honest.

Mr Hyde's house was in a grim and dingy street, where many ragged children huddled in doorways, and many people of many nationalities walked past to have a morning glass of alcohol. This was the home of Henry Jekyll's favourite, of a man who was heir to a quarter of a million sterling.

An ivory-faced and silver-haired old woman, with an evil, hypocritical face opened the door. Her manners were excellent. Yes, Mr Hyde did live there, but he was not at home. He had been in that night very late, but had gone away again in less than an hour. There was nothing strange in that, for he had very irregular habits. The lawyer then demanded to see his room, and introduced his companion as Inspector Newcomen of Scotland Yard. A flash of odious joy appeared on the woman's face.

"Ah!" said she. "He is in trouble then! What has he done?"

Exchanging glances, Mr Utterson and the inspector went into the rooms occupied by Mr Hyde. They were furnished with luxury and good taste, but at the moment they showed signs of having been recently and hurriedly ransacked – clothes lay about the floor with their pockets inside out, drawers stood open, and on the hearth was a heap of ashes, as though papers had been burned there. One of these was a chequebook, for the butt end still remained, and behind the door was the other half of the walking stick that had killed the old gentleman.

This clinched the officer's suspicions.

"You may depend upon it, sir," he said to Mr Utterson, "I have him in my hand. He must have lost his head or he would never have left the stick, or above all burned the cheque book. Why, money's life to the man. We have nothing to do but wait for him at the bank."

This last, however, was not so easy, for Mr Hyde had numbered few familiars. His family could not be traced, he had never been photographed, and the few who could describe him differed widely. Only on one point were they agreed, and that was the haunting sense of unexpressed deformity with which the fugitive impressed his beholders.


# Incident of the Letter

It was late in the afternoon when Mr Utterson found his way to Dr Jekyll's door, where he was at once admitted by Poole and led down by the kitchen offices and across a yard which had once been a garden to the building which was indifferently known as the laboratory or the dissecting-rooms. The doctor had bought the house from the heirs of a celebrated surgeon; and his own tastes being chemical rather than anatomical, had changed the destination of the block at the bottom of the garden. It was the first time that the lawyer had been received in that part of his friend's quarters; and he eyed the dingy windowless structure with curiosity, and gazed round with a distasteful sense of strangeness as he crossed the theatre, once crowded with eager students and now lying gaunt and silent, the tables laden with chemical apparatus, and the light falling dimly through the foggy cupola. At the farther end, a flight of stairs mounted to a door covered with red baize; and through this, Mr Utterson was at last received into the doctor's cabinet. The fire burned in the grate; a lamp was set lighted on the chimney-shelf, for even in the houses the fog began to lie thickly; and there, close up to the warmth, sat Dr Jekyll, looking deadly sick. He did not rise to meet his visitor, but held out a cold hand, and bade him welcome in a changed voice.

"And now," said Mr Utterson, "you have heard the news?"

The doctor shuddered. "They were crying it in the square," he said. "I heard them in my dining-room."

"One word," said the lawyer. "You have not been mad enough to hide this fellow?"

"Utterson, I swear to God," cried the doctor, "I swear to God I will never set eyes on him again. It is all at an end. And indeed he does not want my help; you do not know him as I do; he is safe, he is quite safe; mark my words, he will never more be heard of. But there is one thing on which you may advise me. I have – I have received a letter; and I am at a loss whether I should show it to the police."

The letter was written in an odd, upright hand, and signed "Edward Hyde"; and it signified, briefly enough, that the writer's benefactor, Dr Jekyll, need labour under no alarm for his safety, as he had means of escape on which he placed a sure dependence. The lawyer liked this letter well enough: it put a better colour on the intimacy than he had looked for; and he blamed himself for some of his past suspicions.

"Well, I shall consider," returned the lawyer. "And now one word more: it was Hyde who dictated the terms in your will about that disappearance?"

The doctor seemed seized with a qualm of faintness; he shut his mouth tight and nodded.

"I knew it," said Utterson. "He meant to murder you. You have had a fine escape."

"I have had what is far more to the purpose," returned the doctor solemnly. "I have had a lesson – O God, Utterson, what a lesson I have had!"

On his way out, the lawyer stopped and had a word or two with Poole. "By the by," said he, "there was a letter handed in today: what was the messenger like?"

But Poole was positive nothing had come except by post. "And only circulars by that," he added.

This news sent off the visitor with his fears renewed. Plainly the letter had come by the laboratory door; possibly indeed it had been written in the cabinet, and if that were so, it must be differently judged and handled with the more caution. The news-boys as he went were crying themselves hoarse along the footways: "Special edition. Shocking murder of an MP." That was the funeral oration of one friend and client, and he could not help a certain apprehension lest the good name of another should be sucked down into the eddy of the scandal. It was at least a ticklish decision that he had to make, and self-reliant as he was by habit, he began to cherish a longing for advice. It was not to be had directly, but perhaps, he thought, it might be fished for.

Presently after, Mr Utterson sat on one side of his own hearth, with Mr Guest, his head clerk, upon the other, and midway between, at a nicely calculated distance from the fire, a bottle of particular old wine. Insensibly the lawyer melted. There was no man from whom he kept fewer secrets than Mr Guest. Guest had often been on business to the doctor's: he knew Poole; he could scarce have failed to hear of Mr Hyde's familiarity about the house; he might draw conclusions. Was it not as well, then, that he should see a letter which put that mystery to right? And, above all, since Guest, being a great student and critic of handwriting, would consider the step natural and obliging? The clerk, besides, was a man of counsel; he would scarce read so strange a document without dropping a remark; and by that remark Mr Utterson might shape his course.

"This is a sad business about Sir Danvers," he said.

"Yes, sir, indeed," returned Guest. "The man, of course, was mad."

"I should like to hear your views on that," replied Utterson. "I have a document here in his handwriting; it is between ourselves, for it is an ugly business at the best. But there it is; a murderer's autograph."

Guest's eyes brightened, and he sat down at once and studied it with passion. "No, sir," he said; "not mad; but it is an odd hand."

"And by all accounts a very odd writer," added the lawyer.

Just then the servant entered with a note.

"Is that from Dr Jekyll, sir?" inquired the clerk. "I thought I knew the writing. Anything private, Mr Utterson?"

"Only an invitation to dinner. Why? Do you want to see it?"

"One moment. I thank you, sir." The clerk laid the two sheets of paper alongside and sedulously compared their contents. "Thank you, sir," he said at last, returning both; "it's a very interesting autograph."

There was a pause during which Mr Utterson struggled with himself. "Why did you compare them, Guest?" he inquired suddenly.

"Well, sir," returned the clerk, "there's a rather singular resemblance; the two hands are in many points identical: only differently sloped."

"Rather quaint," said Utterson.

"It is, as you say, rather quaint," returned Guest.

But no sooner was Mr Utterson alone that night than he locked the note into his safe, where it reposed from that time forward. "What!" he thought. "Henry Jekyll forge for a murderer!" And his blood ran cold in his veins.

# Remarkable Incident of Dr Lanyon

Time ran on; thousands of pounds were offered in reward, for the death of Sir Danvers was resented as a public injury; but Mr Hyde had disappeared out of the ken of the police as though he had never existed. Much of his past was unearthed, indeed, and all disreputable: tales came out of the man's cruelty, at once so callous and violent, of his vile life, of his strange associates, of the hatred that seemed to surround his career; but of his present whereabouts not a whisper. From the time he had left his house in Soho on the morning of the murder, he was simply blotted out, and to Mr Utterson's way of thinking the death of Sir Danvers Carew was more than paid for by the disappearance of Mr Hyde. Now that that evil influence had been withdrawn, a new life began for Dr Jekyll. He came out of his seclusion, renewed relations with his friends, became once more their familiar guest and entertainer; his face seemed to open and brighten, as if with an inward consciousness of service; and for more than two months, the doctor was at peace.

On the 8th of January Utterson had dined at the doctor's with a small party; Lanyon had been there; and the face of the host had looked from one to the other as in the old days when the trio were inseparable friends. On the 12th, and again on the 14th, the door was shut against the lawyer. On the 15th, he tried again, and was again refused; and having now been used for the last two months to see his friend almost daily, he found this return of solitude to weigh upon his spirits. The fifth night, he had Mr Guest to dine with him; and the sixth he betook himself to Dr Lanyon's.

There at least he was not denied admittance; but when he came in, he was shocked at the change which had taken place in the doctor's appearance. He had his death-warrant written legibly upon his face. And yet when Utterson remarked on his ill looks, it was with an air of great firmness that Lanyon declared himself a doomed man.

"I have had a shock," he said, "and I shall never recover. It is a question of weeks. Well, life has been pleasant; I liked it; yes, sir, I used to like it. I sometimes think if we knew all, we should be more glad to get away."

"Jekyll is ill, too," observed Utterson. "Have you seen him?"

But Lanyon's face changed, and he held up a

trembling hand. "I wish to see or hear no more of Dr Jekyll," he said, in a loud, unsteady voice. "I am quite done with that person; and I beg that you will spare me any allusion to one whom I regard as dead."

As soon as he got home, Utterson sat down and wrote to Jekyll, complaining of his exclusion from the house, and asking the cause of this unhappy break with Lanyon; and the next day brought him a long answer, often very pathetically worded, and sometimes darkly mysterious in drift. The quarrel with Lanyon was incurable.

"I do not blame our old friend," Jekyll wrote, "but I share his view that we must never meet. I mean henceforth to lead a life of extreme seclusion: you must not be surprised, nor must you doubt my friendship, if my door is often shut even to you. You must suffer me to go my own dark way. I have brought on myself a punishment and a danger I cannot name. If I am the chief of sinners, I am also the chief of sufferers. I could not think that this earth contained a place for suffering and terrors so unmanning, and you can do but one thing, Utterson, to lighten this destiny, and that is to respect my silence."

A week afterwards Dr Lanyon took to his bed, and in something less than a fortnight he was dead. The night after the funeral, Utterson locked the door of his business room, and drew out an envelope addressed; "PRIVATE: for the hands of J. G. Utterson ALONE, and in case of his pre-decease *to be destroyed unread*". Within there was another enclosure, likewise sealed, and marked upon the cover as "not to be opened till the death or disappearance of Dr Henry Jekyll". A great curiosity came to the trustee, but professional honour and faith to his dead friend were stringent obligations; and the packet slept in the inmost corner of his private safe.

## Incident at the Window

It chanced one Sunday, when Mr Utterson was on his usual walk with Mr Enfield, that their way lay once again through the by-street; and that when they came in front of the door, both stopped to gaze on it.

"Well," said Enfield, "that story's at an end, at least. We shall never see more of Mr Hyde."

"I hope not," said Utterson. "Did I ever tell you that I once saw him, and shared your feeling of repulsion?"

"It was impossible to do the one without the other," returned Enfield. "And, by the way, what an ass you must have thought me, not to know that this was a back way to Dr Jekyll's!"

"So you found it out, did you?" said Utterson. "But if that be so, we may step into the court and take a look at the windows. To tell you the truth, I am uneasy about poor Jekyll; and even outside I feel as if a friend might do him good."

The middle one of the three windows was half-way open; and sitting close beside it, taking the air with an infinite sadness of mien, like some disconsolate prisoner, Utterson saw Dr Jekyll.

"What! Jekyll!" he cried. "I trust you are better."

"I am very low, Utterson," replied the doctor drearily; "very low. It will not last long, thank God."

"You stay too much indoors," said the lawyer. "You should be out, whipping up the circulation, like Mr Enfield and me. Come now; get your hat, and take a quick turn with us."

"You are very good," sighed the other. "I should like to very much; but no, no, no; it is quite impossible; I dare not. But indeed, Utterson, I am very glad to see you; this is really a great pleasure. I would ask you and Mr Enfield up, but the place is really not fit."

"Why then," said the lawyer, good-naturedly, "the best thing we can do is to stay down here, and speak with you from where we are."

"That is just what I was about to venture to propose," returned the doctor, with a smile. But the words were hardly uttered, before the smile was struck out of his face and succeeded by an expression of such abject terror and despair, as froze the very blood of the two gentlemen below. They saw it but for a glimpse, for the window was instantly thrust down; but that glimpse had been sufficient, and they turned and left the court without a word. In silence, too, they traversed the by-street; and it was not until they had come into a neighbouring thoroughfare that Mr Utterson at last turned and looked at his companion. They were both pale; and there was an answering horror in their eyes.

"God forgive us! God forgive us!" said Mr Utterson.

## The Last Night

Mr Utterson was sitting by his fireside one evening after dinner, when he was surprised to receive a visit from Poole.

"Bless me, Poole, what brings you here?" he cried; and then, taking a second look at him, "What ails you?" he added; "is the doctor ill?"

"Mr Utterson," said the man, "there is something wrong. I've been afraid for about a week, and I can bear it no more. I think there's been foul play."

"Foul play!" cried the lawyer, a good deal frightened, and rather inclined to be irritated in consequence. "What foul play?"

"I daren't say, sir," was the answer; "but will you come along with me and see for yourself?"

It was a wild, cold , seasonable night of March, with a pale moon, lying on her back as though the wind had tilted her, and a flying wrack of the most diaphanous and lawny texture. The wind made talking difficult, and flecked the blood into the face. It seemed to have swept the streets unusually bare of passengers, besides, for Mr Utterson thought he had never seen that part of London so deserted. He could have wished it otherwise; never in his life had he been so conscious of so sharp a wish to see and touch his fellow-creatures; for, struggle as he might, there was borne in upon his mind a crushing anticipation of calamity. The square, when they got there, was all full of wind and dust, and the thin trees in the garden were lashing themselves along the railing. Poole now pulled up in the middle of the pavement and in spite of the biting wind took off his hat and mopped his brow with a red pocket handkerchief. But for all the hurry of his coming, these were not the dews of exertion that he wiped away, but the moisture of some strangling anguish – for his face was white, and his voice when he spoke, harsh and broken.

When they reached Jekyll's house, Poole knocked in a very guarded manner; the door opened on the chain; and a voice asked from within, "Is that you, Poole?"

"It's all right," said Poole. "Open the door."

The hall, when they entered it, was brightly lighted up; the fire was built high; and about the hearth the whole of the servants, men and women, stood huddled together like a flock of sheep.

"They're all afraid," said Poole. And then he begged Mr Utterson to follow him, and led the way to the back gardens.

"Now, sir," said he, "you come as gently as you can. I want you to hear, and I don't want you to be heard. And see here, sir, if by any chance he was to ask you in, don't go. Mr Utterson, sir, asking to see you," he called.

A voice answered from within. "Tell him I cannot see anyone," it said complainingly.

"Thank you, sir," said Poole, with a note of something like triumph in his voice; and taking up his candle, he led Mr Utterson back across the yard and into the great kitchen.

"Sir," he said, looking Mr Utterson in the eyes, "was that my master's voice? Have I been twenty years in this man's house, to be deceived about his voice? No, sir; master's made away with; he was made away with eight days ago, when we heard him cry out upon the name of God; and *who's* in there instead of him, and *why* it stays there, is a thing that cries to Heaven, Mr Utterson!"

"This is a very strange tale, Poole," said Mr Utterson, biting his finger. "Suppose it were as you suppose, supposing Dr Jekyll to have been – well, murdered, what could induce the murderer to stay?"

"All this last week, whatever it is that lives in that cabinet has been crying night and day for some sort of medicine and cannot get it to his mind. It was sometimes his way – the master's, that is – to write his orders on a sheet of paper and throw it on the stair. We've had nothing else this week back; nothing but papers, and a closed door, and the very meals left there to be smuggled in when nobody was looking. Well, sir, every day, ay, and twice and thrice in the same day, there have been orders and complaints, and I have been sent flying to all the wholesale chemists in town. Every time I brought the stuff back, there would be another paper telling me to return it, because it was not pure, and another order to a different firm. This drug is wanted bitter bad, sir, whatever for."

"Have you any of these papers?" asked Mr Utterson.

Poole felt in his pocket and handed out a crumpled note, which the lawyer, bending nearer to the candle, carefully examined. At first, the letter had run composedly enough; but then with a sudden splutter of the pen, the writer's emotion had broken loose. "For God's sake," he had added, "find me some of the old."

"This is unquestionably the doctor's hand, do you know?" resumed the lawyer.

"I thought it looked like it," said the servant. "But what matters hand of write? I've seen him!"

"Seen him?" repeated Mr Utterson. "Well?"

"That's it!" said Poole. "It was this way. I came suddenly into the theatre from the garden. It seems he had slipped out to look for this drug, or whatever it is; for the cabinet door was open, and there he was at the far end of the room, digging among the crates. He looked up when I came in, gave a kind of cry, and whipped upstairs into the cabinet. It was but for one minute that I saw him,

39

but the hair stood upon my head like quills. Sir, if that was my master, why had he a mask upon his face? If it was my master, why did he cry out like a rat, and run from me? I have served him long enough. And then . . ."

"These are all very strange circumstances," said Mr Utterson, "but I think I begin to see daylight. Your master, Poole, is plainly seized with one of those maladies that both torture and deform the sufferer; hence, for aught I know, the alteration of his voice; hence the mask and his avoidance of his friends; hence his eagerness to find this drug by means of which the poor soul retains some hope of ultimate recovery – God grant that he be not deceived! There is my explanation, Poole – it is sad enough, and appalling to consider, but it is plain and natural, hangs well together, and delivers us all from exhorbitant alarms."

The man paused, and passed his hand over his face. "That thing was not my master, and there's the truth. My master" – here he looked round him, and began to whisper – "is a tall fine build of a man, and this was more of a dwarf."

"It is well, then, that we should be frank," said the other. "We both think more than we have said; let us make a clean breast. This masked figure that you saw, did you recognise it?"

"Well, sir, it went so quick, and the creature was so doubled up, that I could hardly swear to that," was the answer. "But if you mean, was it Mr Hyde? – why, yes, I think it was! There was something queer about that gentleman – something that gave a man a turn – I don't know rightly how to say it, sir, beyond this: that you felt it in your marrow – kind of cold and thin."

"I own I felt something of what you describe," said Mr Utterson.

"Quite so, sir," returned Poole. "Well, when that masked thing like a monkey jumped from among the chemicals and whipped into the cabinet, it went down my spine like ice."

"Evil, I fear, founded – evil was sure to come of – that connection. Ay, truly, I believe you; I believe poor Harry is killed; and I believe his murderer (for what purpose, God alone can tell) is still lurking in his victim's room. Well, let our name be vengeance. Call Bradshaw."

The footman came at the summons, very white and nervous.

"Pull yourself together, Bradshaw," said the lawyer. "This suspense, I know, is telling upon all of you; but it is now our intention to make an end of it. Poole, here, and I are going to force our way into the cabinet. If all is well, my shoulders are broad enough to bear the blame. Meanwhile, lest anything should really be amiss, or any malefactor seek to escape by the back, you and the boy must go round the corner with a pair of good sticks, and take your post at the laboratory door.

"Jekyll," cried Utterson, with a loud voice, "I demand to see you." He paused a moment, but there came no reply. "I give you fair warning, our suspicions are aroused, and I must and shall see

41

you," he resumed; "if not by fair means, then by foul – if not of your consent, then by brute force!"

"Utterson," said the voice, "for God's sake, have mercy!"

"Ah, that's not Jekyll's voice – it's Hyde's!" cried Utterson. "Down with the door, Poole!"

Poole swung the axe over his shoulder; the blow shook the building, and the red baize door leaped against the lock and hinges. A dismal screech, as of mere animal terror, rang from the cabinet. Up went the axe again, and again the panels crashed and the frame bounded; four times the blow fell; but the wood was tough and the fittings were of excellent workmanship; and it was not until the fifth, that the lock burst in sunder, and the wreck of the door fell inwards on the carpet.

There lay the body of a man sorely contorted and still twitching. They drew near on tiptoe, turned it on his back, and beheld the face of Edward Hyde. He was dressed in clothes far too large for him, clothes of the doctor's bigness; the cords of his face still moved with a semblance of life, but life was quite gone; and by the crushed phial in the hand and the strong smell of kernels that hung upon the air, Utterson knew that he was looking on the body of a self-destroyer. Nowhere was there any trace of Henry Jekyll, dead or alive.

On the desk among the neat array of papers, a large envelope was uppermost, and bore, in the doctor's hand, the name of Mr Utterson. The lawyer unsealed it, and several enclosures fell to

the floor. The first was a will, drawn in the same eccentric terms as the one which he had returned six months before, to serve as a testament in case of death and as a deed of gift in case of disappearance; but in place of the name of Edward Hyde, the lawyer, with indescribable amazement, read the name of Gabriel John Utterson.

He caught the next paper; it was a brief note in the doctor's hand, and dated at the top. "Oh, Poole!" the lawyer cried. "He was alive and here this day." And with that he brought the paper to his eyes, and read as follows:

> "MY DEAR UTTERSON, When this shall fall into your hands, I shall have disappeared, under what circumstances I have not the penetration to foresee; but my instincts and all the circumstances of my nameless situation tell me that the end is sure and must be early. Go then, and first read the narrative which Lanyon warned me he was to place in your hands; and if you care to hear more, turn to the confession of
>
> Your unworthy and unhappy friend,
>
> HENRY JEKYLL."

"There was a third enclosure?" asked Utterson.

"Here, sir," said Poole, and gave into his hands a considerable packet sealed in several places.

They went out, locking the door of the theatre behind them; and Utterson, once more leaving the servants gathered about the fire in the hall, trudged back to his office to read the two narratives in which this mystery was now to be explained.

# Dr Lanyon's Narrative

On the ninth of January, now four days ago, I received a registered envelope from Henry Jekyll. This is how the letter ran:

"10*th December,* 18—
DEAR LANYON, You are one of my oldest friends; and although we may have differed at times on scientific questions, I cannot remember, at least on my side, any break in our affection. Lanyon, my life, my honour, my reason, are all at your mercy; if you fail me to-night, I am lost.

I want you to postpone all other engagements for tonight and, with this letter in your hand for consultation, to drive straight to my house. Poole, my butler, has his orders; you will find him waiting your arrival with a locksmith. The door of my cabinet is then to be forced; and you are to go in alone; to open the glazed press and to draw out, *with all its contents as they stand,* the fourth drawer from the top. You may know the right drawer by its contents: some powders, a phial, and a paper book. This drawer I beg of you to carry back with you to Cavendish Square exactly as it stands.

At midnight, I have to ask you to be alone in your consulting-room, to admit with your own hand into the house a man who will present himself in my name, and to place in his hands the drawer that you will have brought with you from my cabinet. Then you will have played your part, and earned my gratitude completely.

Serve me, my dear Lanyon, and save

Your friend, H.J."


I felt bound to do as he requested. I rose accordingly from table, got into a hansom, and drove straight to Jekyll's house. The butler was awaiting my arrival; he had received by the same post as mine a registered letter of instruction, and had sent at once for a locksmith and a carpenter. After two hours' work, the door stood open. I proceeded to examine the contents of the drawer. The powders were neatly enough made up, but not with the nicety of the dispensing chemist, so that it was plain that they were of Jekyll's own manufacture. The phial to which I next turned my attention was about half full of a blood-red liquor, which was highly pungent to the sense of smell and seemed to me to contain phosphorus and some volatile ether. At the other ingredients I could make no guess. The book contained little but a series of dates. These covered a period of many years, but I observed that the entries ceased a year ago and quite abruptly. All this, although it whetted my curious nature, told me little that was definite. How could the presence of these articles in my house affect the honour, the sanity or the life of my flighty colleague? I took out the drawer, had it filled up with straw and tied in a sheet, and returned with it to Cavendish Square.

Twelve o'clock had scarce rung out over London, ere the knocker sounded very gently on the door. I went myself at the summons, and found a small man crouching against the pillars of the portico.

"Are you come from Dr Jekyll?" I asked.

He told me "yes" by a constrained gesture; and when I had bidden him enter, he did not obey me without a searching backward glance into the darkness of the square.

This person was dressed in a fashion that would have made an ordinary person laughable; his clothes were enormously too large for him in every measurement – the trousers hanging on his legs and rolled up, the waist of the coat below his haunches, and the collar sprawling wide upon his shoulders. Strange to relate, this was far from moving me to laughter. Rather, as there was something abnormal and misbegotten in the very essence of the creature that now faced me – something seizing, surprising and revolting – this fresh disparity seemed but to fit in with and to reinforce it. My visitor was on fire with sombre excitement.

"Have you got it?" he cried. "Have you got it?" And he laid his hand upon my arm and sought to shake me.

I put him back, conscious at his touch of a certain icy pang along my blood. "Come, sir," said I. "You forget that I have not yet the pleasure of your acquaintance. Be seated, if you please."

"I beg your pardon, Dr Lanyon," he replied, civilly enough. "I come here at the instance of your colleague, Dr Henry Jekyll, on a piece of business of some moment; and I understood . . ." He paused, and put his hand to his throat, and I could see, in spite of his collected manner, that he was wrestling against the approaches of the hysteria, "I understood, a drawer . . ."

"There it is, sir," said I, pointing to it.

He sprang to it, and then paused, and laid his hand upon his heart; I could hear his teeth grate with the convulsive action of his jaws; and his face was so ghastly to see that I grew alarmed both for his life and reason.

"Compose yourself," said I.

He turned a dreadful smile to me, and plucked away the sheet. At sight of the contents, he uttered one loud sob of such immense relief that I sat petrified. "Have you a graduated glass?" he asked.

I rose from my place with something of an effort, and gave him what he asked.

He thanked me, measured out the red tincture and added one of the powders. The mixture, which was at first a reddish hue, began to brighten in

48

colour, to effervesce audibly, and to throw off small fumes of vapour. Suddenly, the compound changed to a dark purple, which faded again more slowly to a watery green. My visitor set down the glass upon the table, and then turned and looked upon me with an air of scrutiny.

"And now," said he, "to settle what remains. Will you suffer me to take this glass in my hand, and to go forth from your house without further parley? Or has the greed of curiosity too much command of you? Think before you answer, for it shall be done as you decide."

"Sir," said I, affecting a coolness that I was far from truly possessing, "I have gone too far in the way of inexplicable service to pause before I see the end."

"It is well," replied my visitor. "Lanyon, you remember your vows: what follows is under the seal of our profession. And now – behold!"

He put the glass to his lips, and drank at one gulp. A cry followed; he reeled, staggered, clutched at the table and held on, staring with injected eyes, gasping with open mouth; and as I looked, there came, I thought, a change – he seemed to swell – his face became suddenly black, and the features seemed to melt and alter – and the next moment I had sprung to my feet and leaped back against the wall, my arm raised to shield me from that prodigy, my mind submerged in terror.

"O God!" I screamed, and, "O God!" again and again; for there before my eyes – pale and shaken, and half-fainting, and groping before him with his hands, like a man restored from death – there stood Henry Jekyll!

What he told me in the next hour I cannot bring my mind to set on paper. I saw what I saw, I heard what I heard, and my soul sickened at it; and yet, now when that sight has faded from my eyes I ask myself if I believe it, and I cannot answer. I will say but one thing, Utterson, and that will be more than enough. The creature who crept into my house that night was, on Jekyll's own confession, known by the name of Hyde and hunted for in every corner of the land as the murderer of Carew.

HASTIE LANYON.

# Henry Jekyll's Full Statement

I was born to a large fortune, inclined by nature to industry, fond of the respect of the wise and good among my fellow men, and thus, with every guarantee of an honourable and distinguished future. The worst of my faults was a certain impatient gaiety of disposition, such as has made the happiness of many, but such as I found it hard to reconcile with my imperious desire to carry my head high, and wear a more than commonly grave countenance before the public. Many a man would have even blazoned such irregularities as I was guilty of; but I regarded and hid them with an almost morbid sense of shame. With every day, and from both sides of my intelligence, the moral and the intellectual, I thus drew steadily nearer to that truth; that man is not truly one, but truly two. I say two, because the state of my own knowledge does not pass beyond that point. I saw that, of the two natures that contended in the field of my consciousness, even if I could rightly be said to be either, it was only because I was radically both; and from an early date, I learned to dwell with pleasure, as a beloved day-dream, on the thought of the separation of these elements. If each, I told myself, could but be housed in separate identities, life would be relieved of all that was unbearable; the unjust might go his way, delivered from the aspirations and remorse of his more upright twin; and the just could walk steadfastly and securely on his upward path, doing the good things in which he found his pleasure, and no longer exposed to disgrace and penitence by the hands of this extraneous evil. How, then, were they dissociated?

For two good reasons, I will not enter deeply into this scientific branch of my confession. First, because I have learned that the doom and burthen of our life is bound for ever on man's shoulders; and when the attempt is made to cast it off, it but returns upon us with more unfamiliar and more awful pressure. Second, because, as my narrative will make, alas! too evident, my discoveries were incomplete. Enough, then, that I managed to compound a drug by which a second form and countenance appeared which bore the stamp of lower elements in my soul.

I hesitated long before I put this theory to the test of practice. But the temptation of a discovery so singular and profound at last overcame the suggestions of alarm. I had long since prepared my tincture; I purchased at once, from a firm of wholesale chemists, a large quantity of a particular salt, which I knew, from my experiments, to be the last ingredient required; and, late one accursed night, I compounded the elements, watched them boil together in the glass, and when the ebullition had subsided, with a strong glow of courage, I drank off the potion.

The most racking pangs succeeded: a grinding in the bones, deadly nausea, and a horror of the spirit that cannot be exceeded at the hour of birth or death. Then these agonies began swiftly to subside, and I came to myself as if out of a great sickness. I felt younger, lighter, happier in body. I knew myself to be more wicked, tenfold more wicked, sold a slave to my original evil; and the thought, in that moment, braced and delighted me like wine. I stretched out my hands, and in the act, I was suddenly aware that I had lost in stature.

There was no mirror, at that date, in my room. I stole through the corridors, a stranger in my own house; and coming to my room, I saw for the first time the appearance of Edward Hyde.

The evil side of my nature was less robust and less developed than the good which I had just

deposed. Again, in the course of my life, which
had been after all, nine-tenths a life of effort,
virtue and control, it had been much less
exercised and much less exhausted. And hence, as
I think, it came about that Edward Hyde was so
much smaller, slighter. and younger than Henry

Jekyll. Evil had left on that body an imprint of deformity and decay. And yet when I looked upon that ugly idol in the glass, I was conscious of no repugnance, rather of a leap of welcome. This, too, was myself. Edward Hyde, alone, in the ranks of mankind, was pure evil.

I lingered but a moment at the mirror: the second and conclusive experiment had yet to be attempted. I once more prepared and drank the cup, once more suffered the pangs of dissolution, and came to myself once more with the character, the stature, and the face of Henry Jekyll.

That night I had come to the fatal cross-roads. Had I approached my discovery in a more noble spirit, had I risked the experiment while under the empire of generous or pious aspirations, all must have been otherwise, and from these agonies of death and birth I had come forth an angel instead of a fiend. The drug had no discriminating action – it but shook the doors of the prison house of my disposition, and that which stood within ran forth. The movement was thus wholly toward the worse.

I had not yet conquered my aversion to the dryness of a life of study. I would still be merrily disposed at times; and as my pleasures were (to say the least) undignified, and I was not only well known and highly considered, but growing towards the elderly man, this incoherency of my life was daily growing more unwelcome. It was on this side that my new power tempted me until I fell in slavery. I had but to drink the cup, to doff at once the body of the noted professor, and to assume, like a thick cloak, that of Edward Hyde. I smiled at the notion; it seemed to me at the time to be humorous; and I made my preparations with the most studious care. And thus fortified, I began to profit by the strange immunities of my position.

The pleasures which I made haste to seek in my disguise were, as I have said, undignified; I would scarce use a harder term. But in the hands of Edward Hyde, they soon began to turn towards the monstrous. When I would come back from these excursions, I was often plunged into a kind of wonder at my vicarious depravity.

Some two months before the murder of Sir Danvers, I had been out for one of my adventures, had returned at a late hour, and woke the next day in bed with somewhat odd sensations. I saw the decent furniture and tall proportions of my room in the square; I recognised the pattern of the bed curtains and the design of the mahogany frame; but something still kept insisting that I was not where I was, that I had not awakened where I seemed to be, but in the little room in Soho where I was accustomed to sleep in the body of Edward Hyde. I smiled to myself, and began lazily to inquire into the elements of this illusion, occasionally, even as I did so, dropping back into a comfortable morning doze. I was still so engaged when, in one of my more wakeful moments, my eye fell upon my hand. The hand which I now saw clearly enough was lean, corded, knuckly, of a dusky pallor, and thickly shaded with a swart growth of hair. It was the hand of Edward Hyde.

Terror woke up in my breast as sudden and startling as the crash of cymbals; and bounding from my bed, I rushed to the mirror. At the sight that met my eyes, my blood was changed into something exquisitely thin and icy. Yes, I had gone to bed Henry Jekyll, I had awakened Edward Hyde. How was this to be explained? I asked myself; and then, with another bound of terror – how was it to be remedied? I had soon dressed, as well as I was able, in clothes of my own size: had soon passed through the house, where Bradshaw stared and drew back at seeing Mr Hyde at such an hour and in such a strange array; and ten minutes later, Dr Jekyll had returned to his own shape, and was sitting down, with a darkened brow, to make a feint of breakfasting.

Small indeed was my appetite. Now, in the light of that morning's accident, I was led to remark that whereas, in the beginning, the difficulty had been to throw off the body of Jekyll, it had of late gradually but decidedly transferred itself to the other side. All things therefore seemed to point to this: that I was slowly losing hold of my original and better self, and becoming slowly incorporated with my second and worse.

Between these two, I now felt I had to choose. To cast in my lot with Jekyll was to die to those appetites which I had long secretly indulged and had of late begun to pamper. To cast it in with Hyde was to die to a thousand interests and aspirations, and to become, at a blow and for ever, despised and friendless. I chose the better part, and was found wanting in the strength to keep it.

I made this choice perhaps with some unconscious reservation, for I neither gave up the house in Soho, nor destroyed the clothes of Edward Hyde, which still lay ready in my cabinet. For two months, however, I was true to my determination. But time began at last to obliterate the freshness of my alarm – the praises of conscience began to grow into a thing of course. I began to be tortured with throes and longings, as of Hyde struggling after freedom; and at last, in an hour of moral weakness, I once again compounded and swallowed the transforming draught.

My devil had been long caged, he came out roaring. I was conscious, even when I took the draught, of a more unbridled, a more furious propensity to ill. It must have been this, I suppose, that stirred in my soul that tempest of impatience with which I listened to the civilities of my unhappy victim; I declare at least, before God, no man morally sane could have been guilty of that crime upon so pitiful a provocation; and that I struck in no more reasonable spirit than that in which a sick child may break a plaything.

Instantly the spirit of hell awoke in me and raged. With a transport of glee, I mauled the unresisting body, tasting delight from every blow; and it was not till weariness had begun to succeed that I was suddenly, in the top fit of my delirium, struck through the heart by a cold thrill of terror. A mist dispersed; I saw my life to be forfeit; and fled from the scene of these excesses. I ran to the house in Soho, and (to make assurance doubly sure) destroyed my papers; thence I set out through the lamplit streets, in the same divided ecstasy of mind, gloating on my crime, light-headedly devising others in the future, and yet still hastening and still hearkening in my wake for the steps of the avenger. Hyde had a song upon his lips as he compounded the draught, and as he drank it pledged the dead man. The pangs of transformation had not done tearing him, before Henry Jekyll, with streaming tears of gratitude and remorse, had fallen upon his knees and lifted his clasped hands to God. The veil of self-indulgence was rent from head to foot. I saw my life as a whole: I followed it up from the days of childhood when I had walked with my father's hand, and through the self-denying toils of my professional life, to arrive again and again, with the same sense of unreality, at the damned horrors of the evening. I could have screamed aloud – I sought with tears and prayers to smother down the crowds of hideous images and sounds with which my memory swarmed against me, and still, between the petitions, the ugly face of my iniquity stared into my soul. As the acuteness of this remorse began to die away, it was succeeded by a sense of joy. The problem of my conduct was solved. Hyde was thenceforth impossible; whether I would or not, I was now confined to the better part of my existence; and, oh, how I rejoiced to think it! with what willing humility I embraced anew the restrictions of natural life! with what sincere renunciation I locked the door by which I had so often gone and come, and ground the key under my heel!

I resolved in my future conduct to redeem the past; and I can say with honesty that my resolve was fruitful of some good. You know yourself how earnestly in the last months of last year I laboured to relieve suffering; you know that much was done for others, and that the days passed quietly, almost happily for myself.

There comes an end to all things. It was a fine, clear January day, and I sat in the sun on a bench. A qualm came over me, a horrid nausea and the most deadly shuddering. These passed away, and left me faint; and then as in its turn the faintness subsided, I began to be aware of a change in the temper of my thoughts, a greater boldness, a contempt of danger, a solution of the bonds of obligation. I looked down; my clothes hung formlessly on my shrunken limbs; the hand that lay on my knee was corded and hairy. I was once more Edward Hyde.

My reason wavered, but it did not fail me utterly. My drugs were in one of the presses of my cabinet: how was I to reach them? That was the problem that (crushing my temples in my hands) I set myself to solve. The laboratory door I had closed. If I sought to enter by the house, my own servants would consign me to the gallows. I saw I must employ another hand, and thought of Lanyon.

When I came to myself at Lanyon's, the horror of my old friend perhaps affected me somewhat: I do not know; it was at least but a drop in the sea to the abhorrence with which I looked back upon these hours. A change had come over me. It was no longer the fear of the gallows, it was the horror of being Hyde that racked me. I came home to my own house and got into bed. I awoke in the morning shaken, weakened. but refreshed.

I was stepping leisurely across the court after breakfast, drinking the chill of the air with pleasure, when I was seized again with those indescribable sensations that heralded the change: and I had but the time to gain the shelter of my cabinet, before I was once again raging and freezing with the passions of Hyde. It took on this occasion a double dose to recall me to myself; and, alas! six hours after, as I sat looking sadly in the fire, the pangs returned, and the drug had to be readministered. In short, from that day forth it seemed only by a great effort as of gymnastics, and only under the immediate stimulation of the drug, that I was able to wear the countenance of Jekyll. If I slept, or even dozed for a moment in my chair, it was always as Hyde that I awakened. Under the strain, I became, in my own person, a creature eaten up and emptied by fever, languidly weak both in mind and body, and solely occupied by one thought: the horror of my other self.

No one has ever suffered such torments; and yet

even to these, habit brought – no, not alleviation – but a certain callousness of soul, a certain acquiescence of despair; and my punishment might have gone on for years, but for the last calamity which has now fallen. My provision of the salt, which had never been renewed since the date of the first experiment, began to run low. I sent out for a fresh supply, and mixed the draught; I drank it, and it was without efficiency. You will learn from Poole how I have had London ransacked; it was in vain; and I am now persuaded that my first supply was impure, and that it was that unknown impurity which lent efficacy to the draught.

About a week has passed, and I am now finishing this statement under the influence of the last of the old powders. This, then, is the last time, short of a miracle, that Henry Jekyll can think his own thoughts or see his own face (now how sadly altered!) in the glass. Half an hour from now, when I shall again and for ever reindue that hated personality, I know how I shall sit shuddering and weeping in my chair, or continue to pace up and down this room (my last earthly refuge) and give ear to every sound of menace. Will Hyde die upon the scaffold? Or will he find the courage to release himself at the last moment? God knows; I am careless; this is my true hour of death, and what is to follow concerns another than myself. Here, then, as I lay down the pen, and proceed to seal up my confession, I bring the life of that unhappy Henry Jekyll to an end.